# BENNY
## AND
# PENNY

### IN
### JUST PRETEND

## GEOFFREY HAYES

# BENNY
## AND
# PENNY

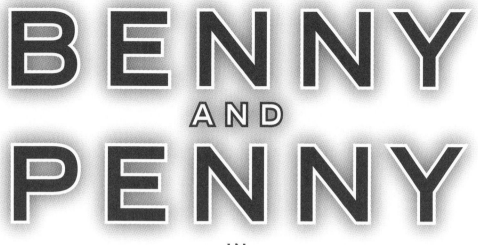

### IN
## JUST PRETEND

### A TOON BOOK BY
# GEOFFREY HAYES

**THE LITTLE LIT LIBRARY,** A DIVISION OF **RAW** JUNIOR, **LLC,** NEW YORK

For Françoise

Editorial Director: FRANÇOISE MOULY
Advisor: ART SPIEGELMAN

Book Design: FRANÇOISE MOULY & JONATHAN BENNETT

 Library of Congress Control Number: 2007941867.

ISBN 13: 978-0-9799238-6-9 ISBN 10: 0-9799238-6-7
Paperback Edition
10 9 8 7 6 5 4 3 2

www.TOON-BOOKS.com

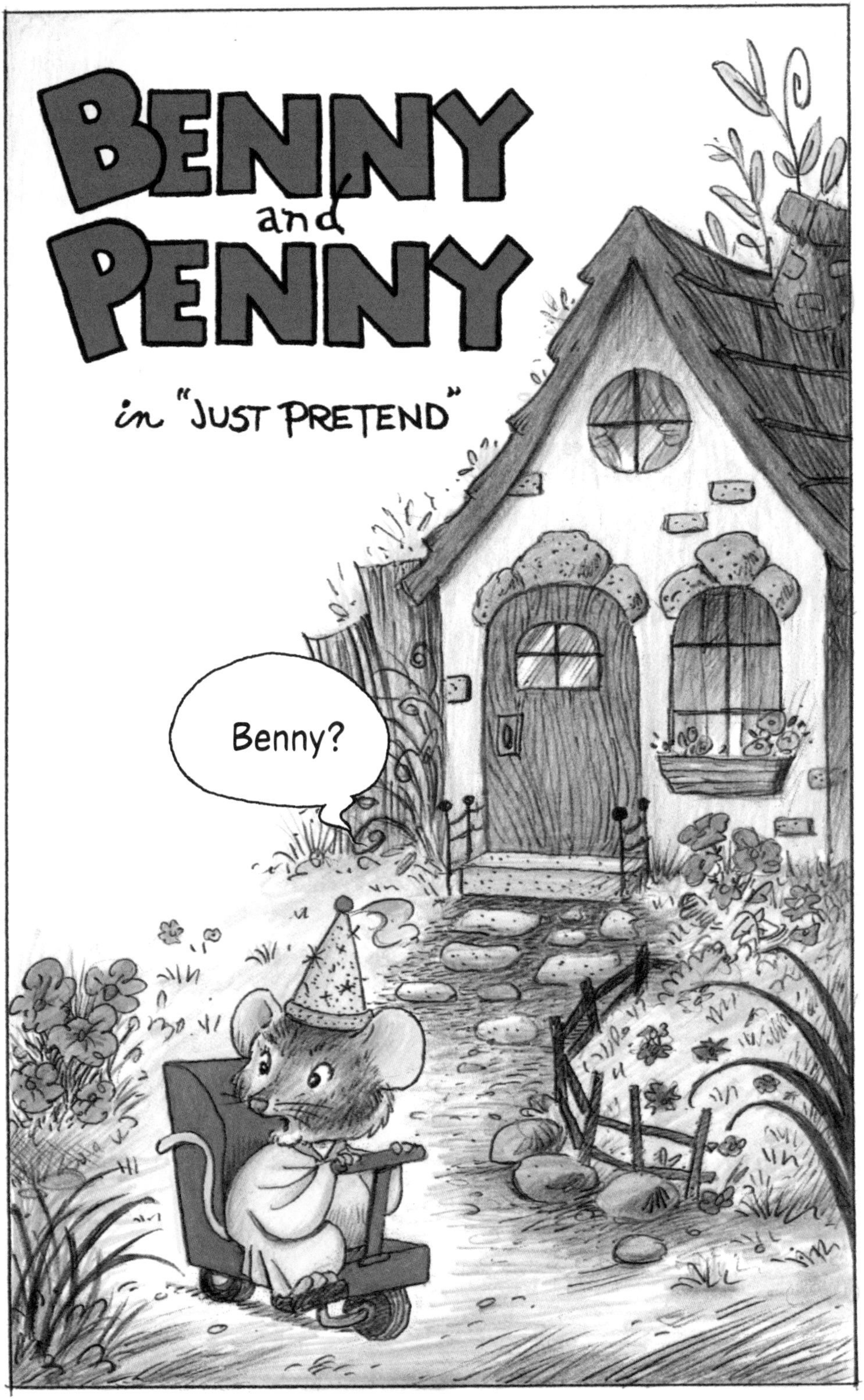
BENNY and PENNY
in "JUST PRETEND"
Benny?

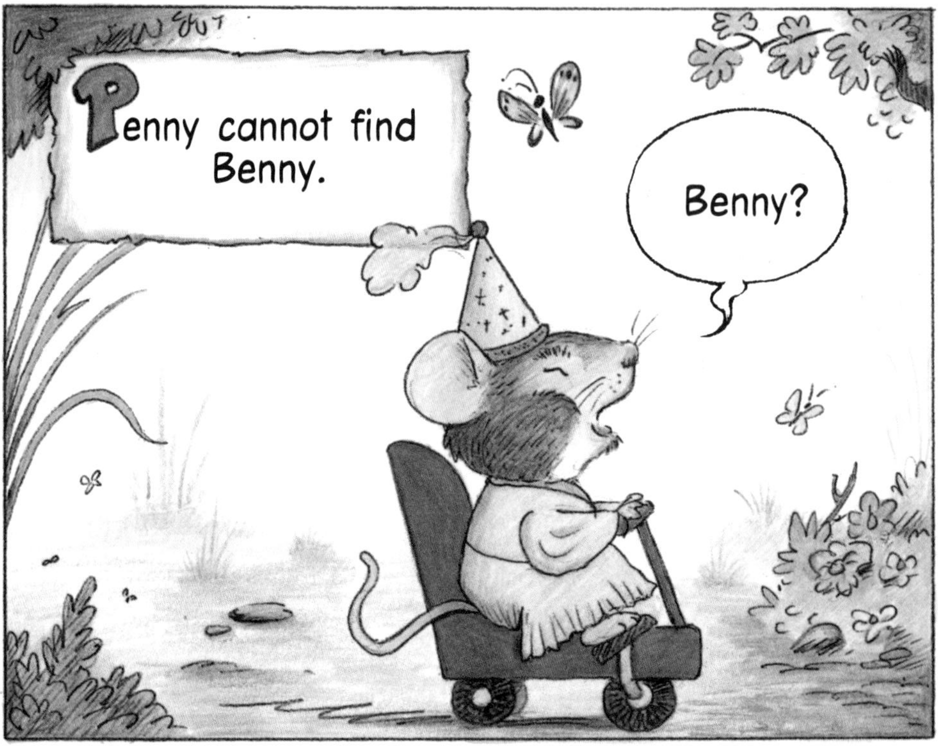
Penny cannot find Benny.
Benny?

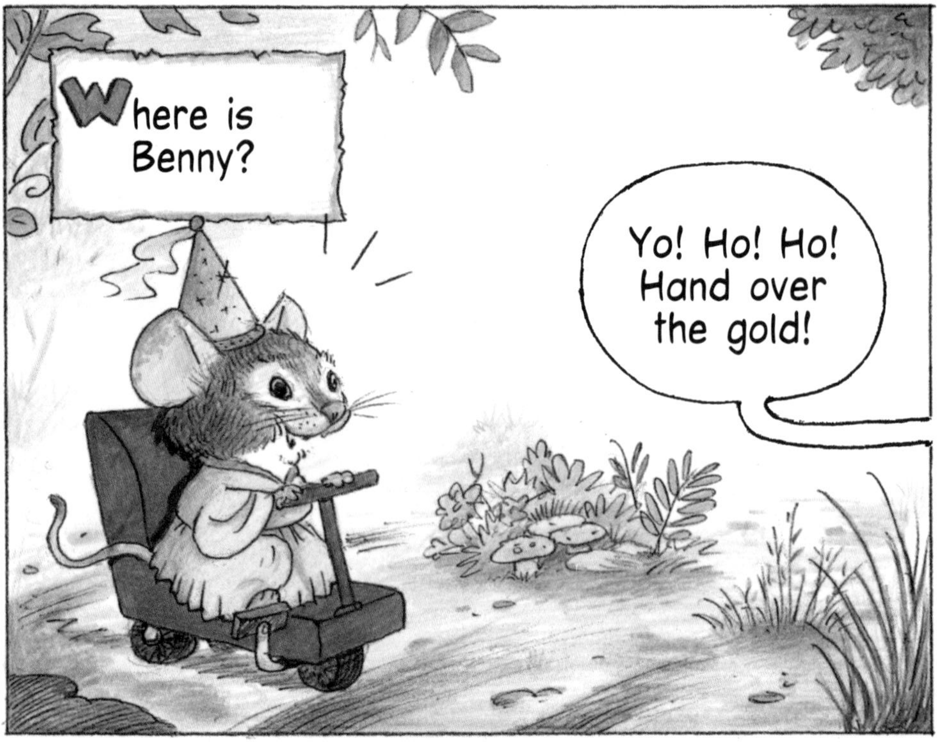
Where is Benny?
Yo! Ho! Ho! Hand over the gold!

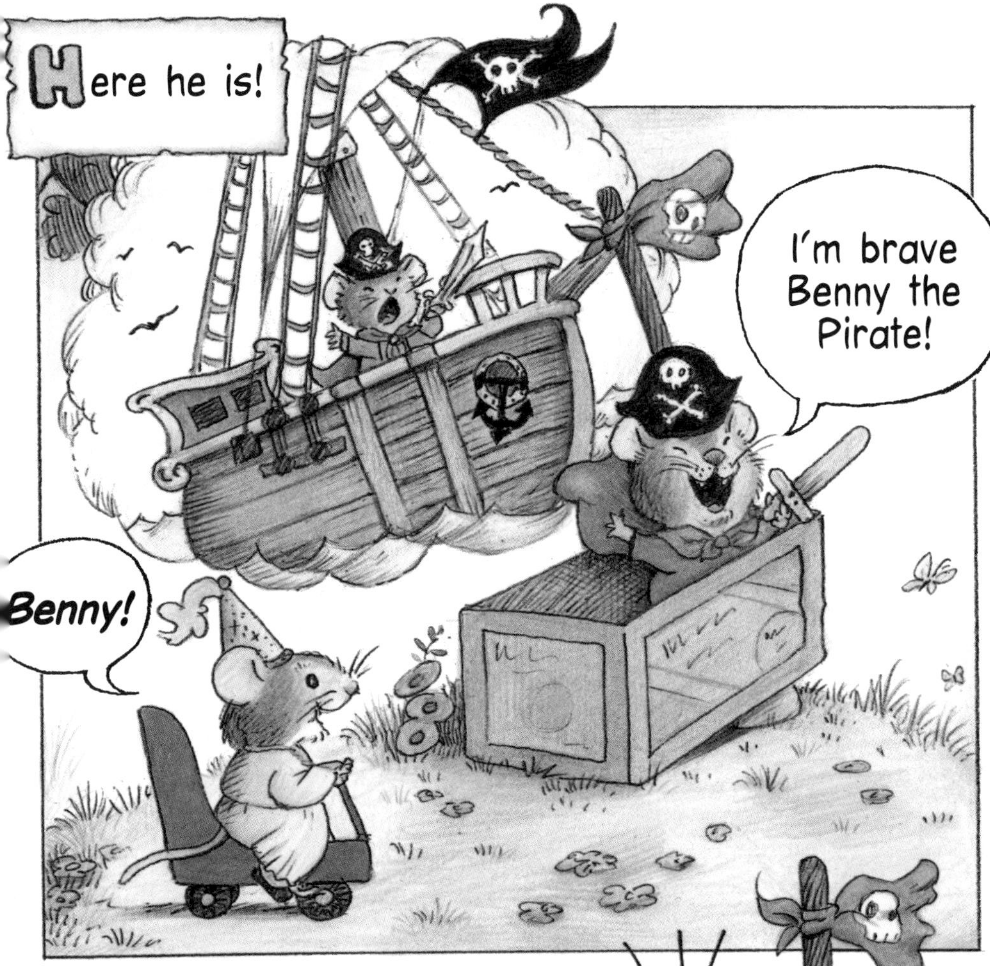
Here he is!
I'm brave Benny the Pirate!
Benny!

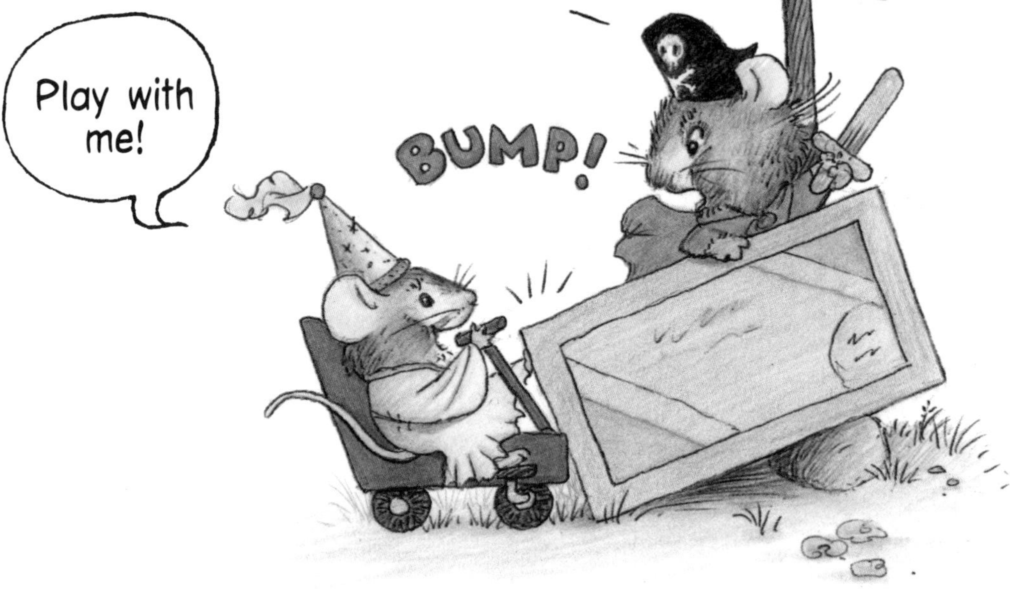
Play with me!
BUMP!

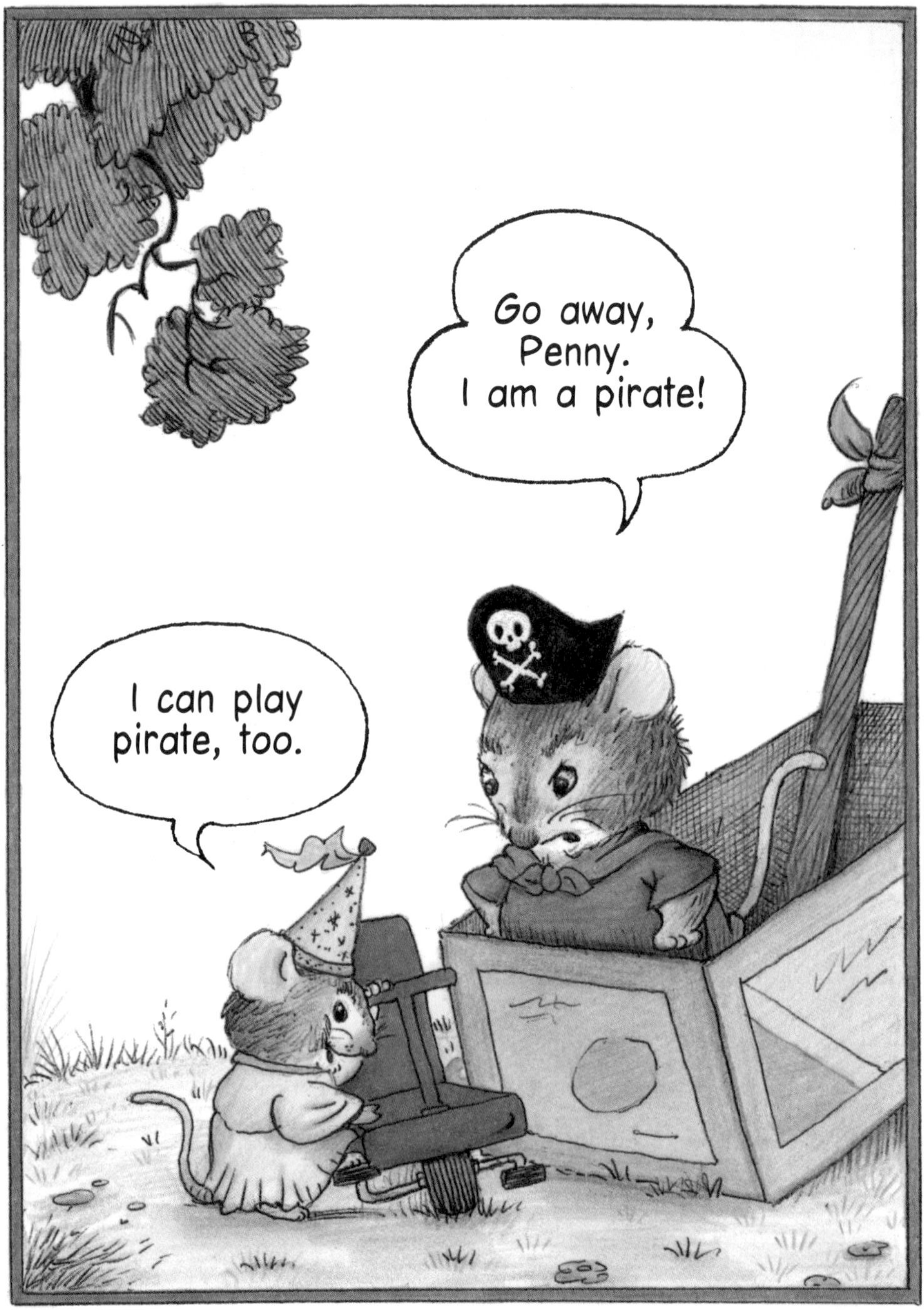
Go away, Penny. I am a pirate!
I can play pirate, too.

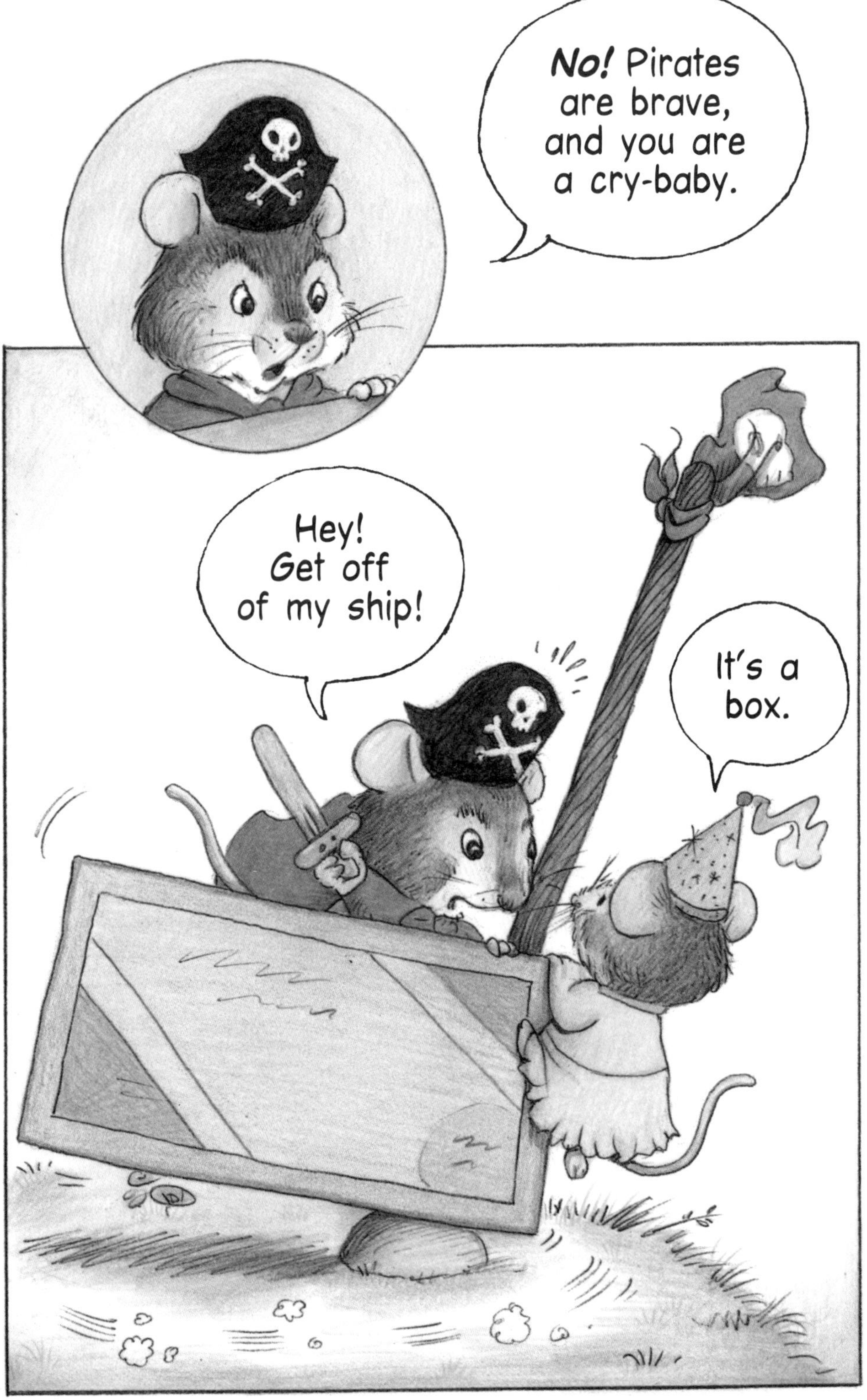
*No!* Pirates are brave, and you are a cry-baby.
Hey! Get off of my ship!
It's a box.

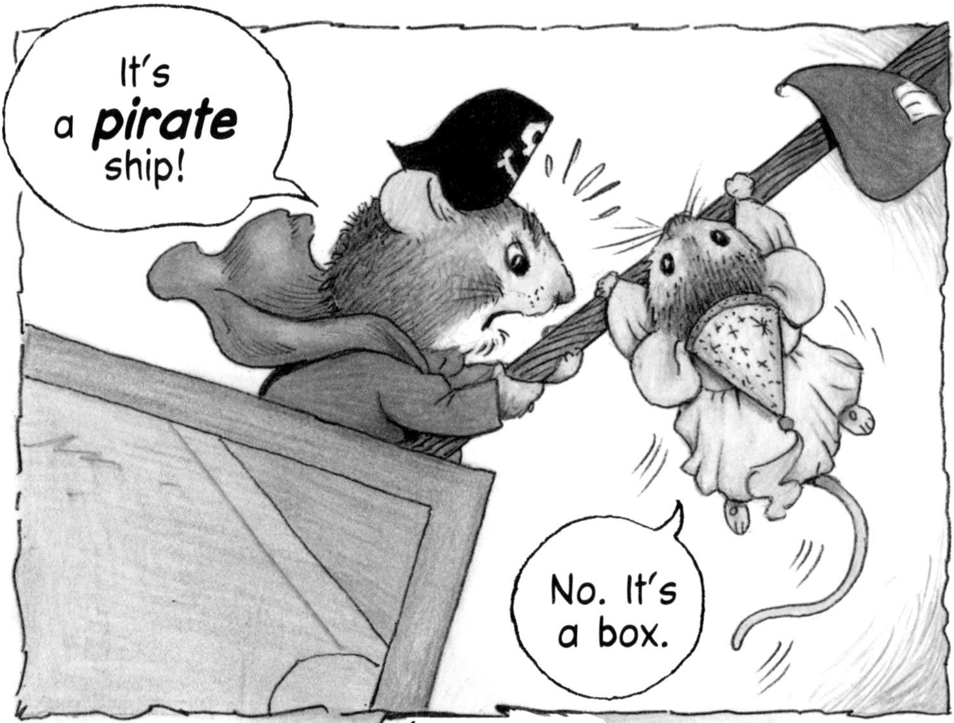
It's a **pirate** ship!
No. It's a box.

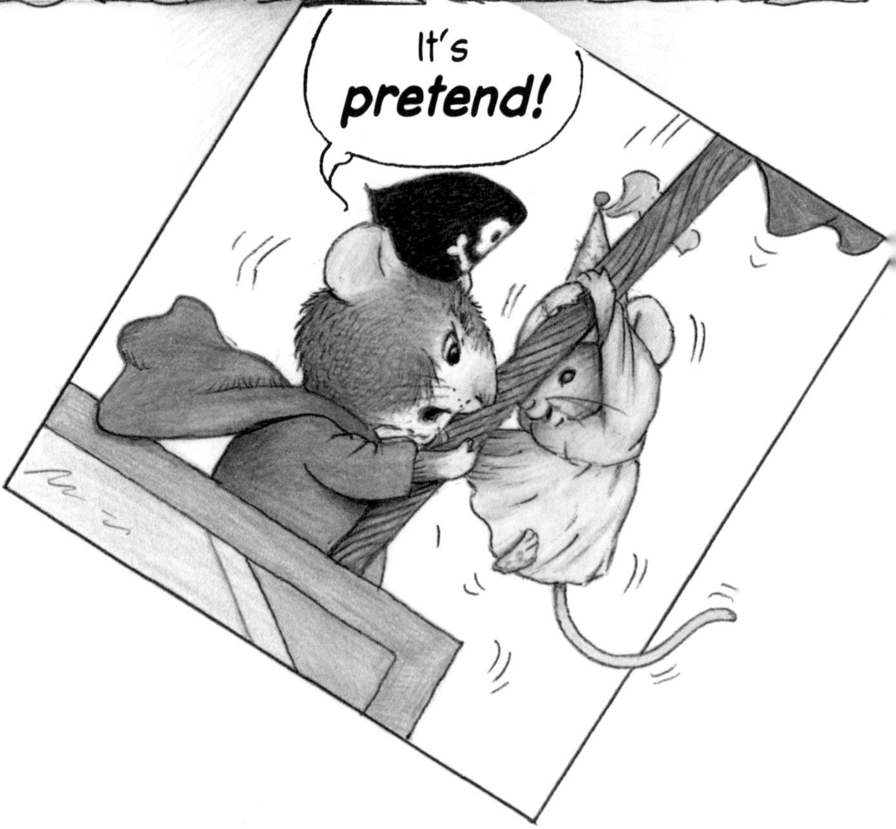
It's **pretend!**

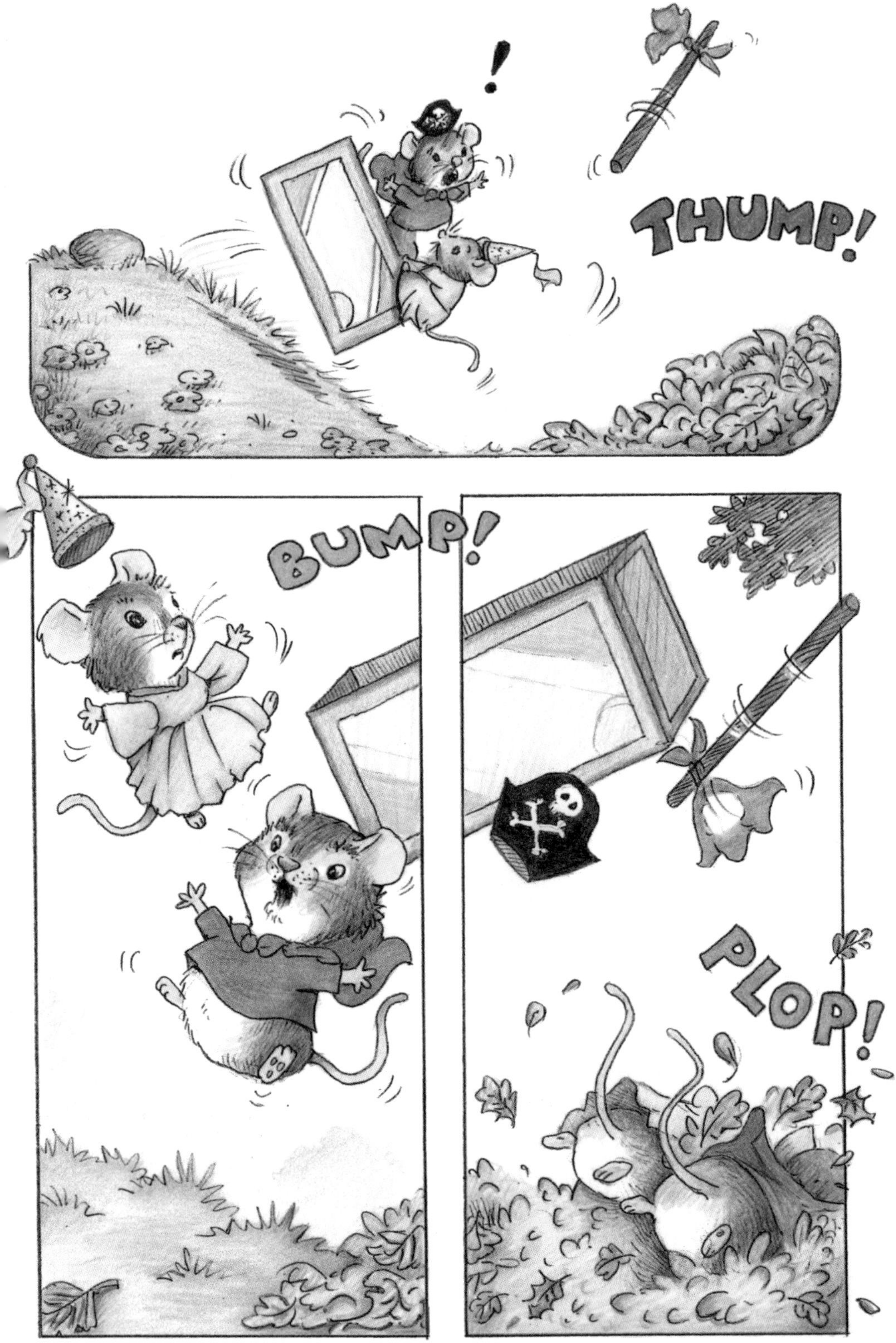
!
THUMP!
BUMP!
PLOP!

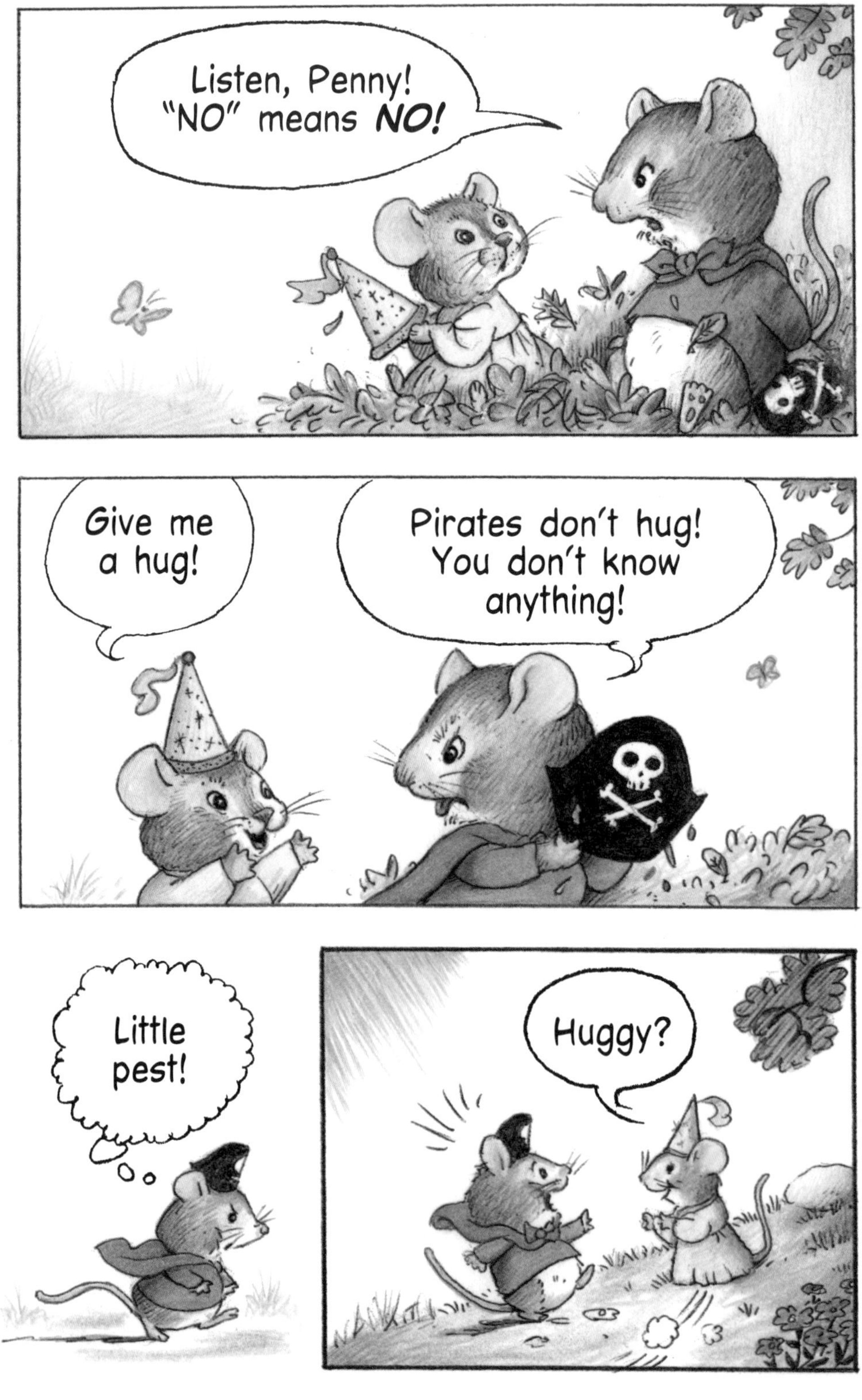
Listen, Penny! "NO" means NO!
Give me a hug!
Pirates don't hug! You don't know anything!
Little pest!
Huggy?

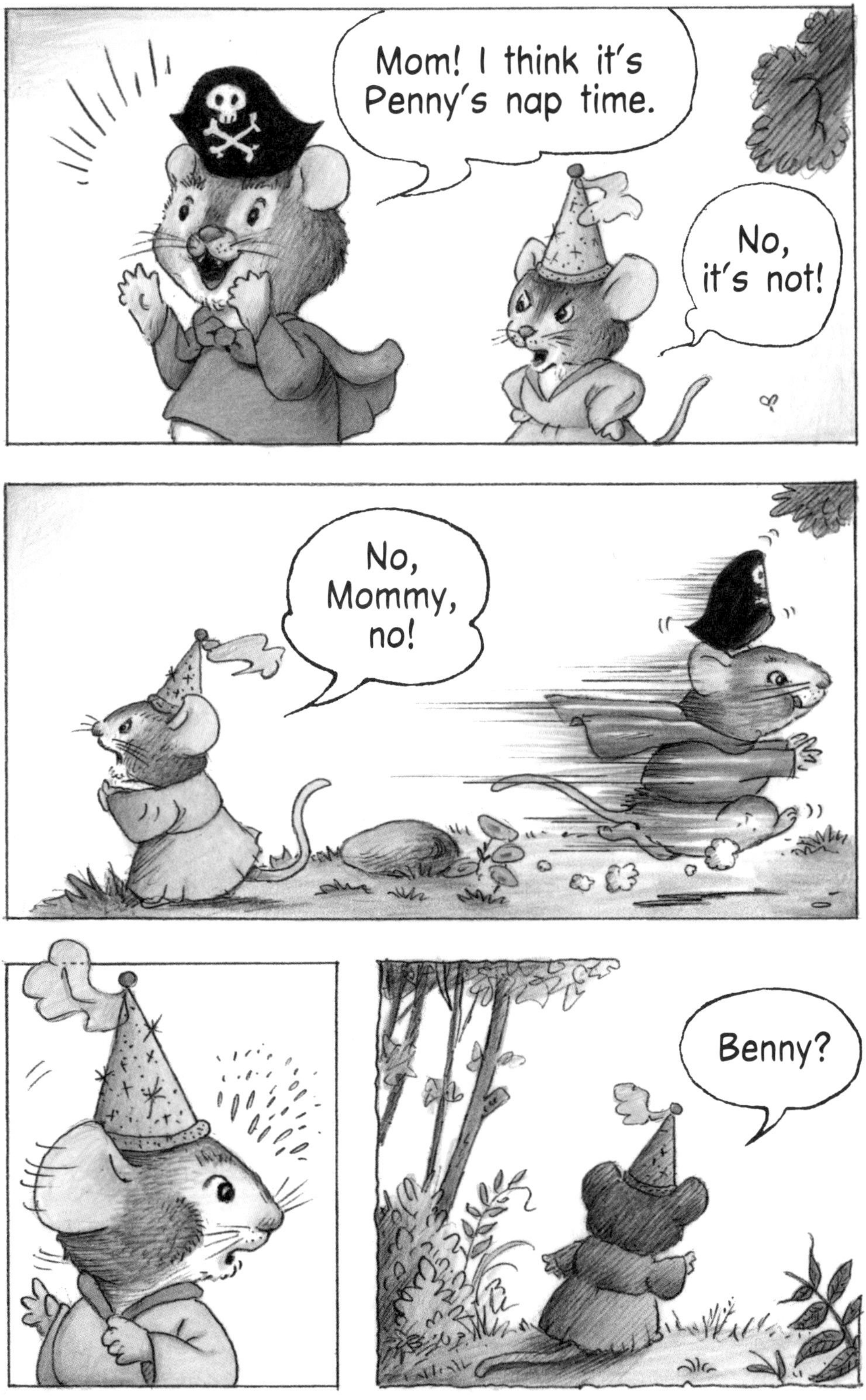
Mom! I think it's Penny's nap time.
No, it's not!
No, Mommy, no!
Benny?

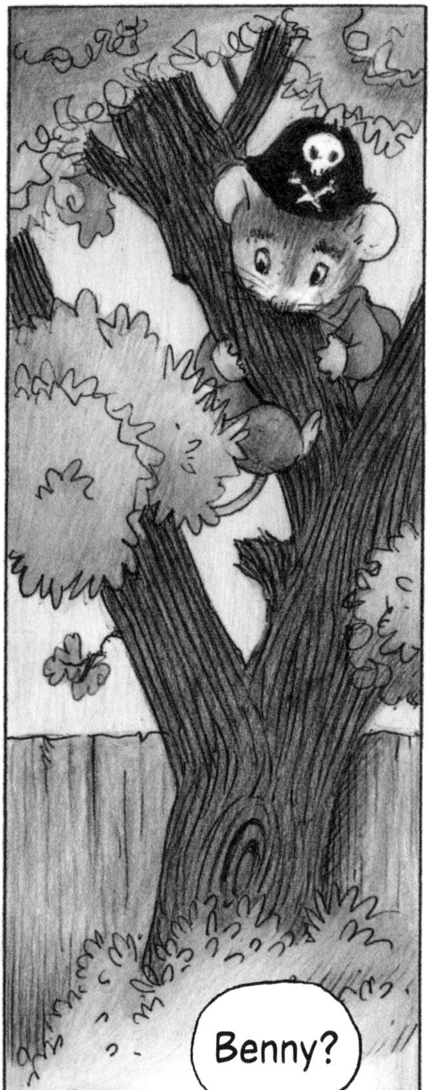
Benny?

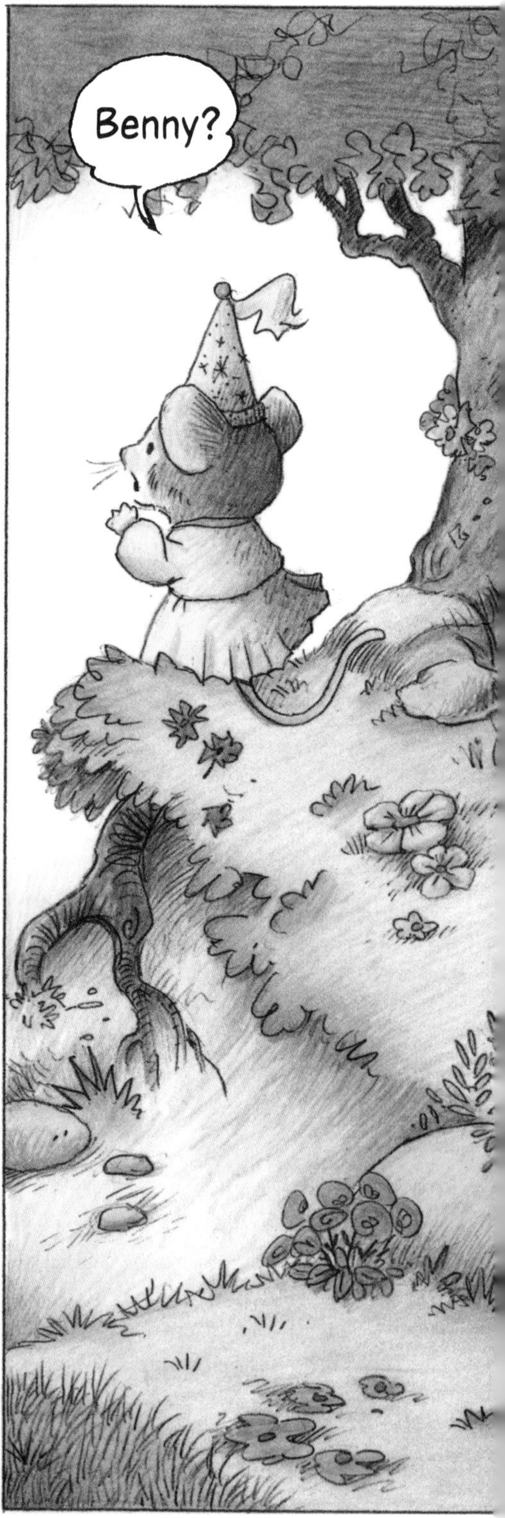
Benny?

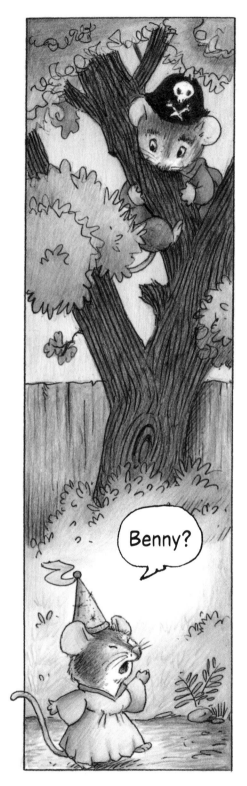

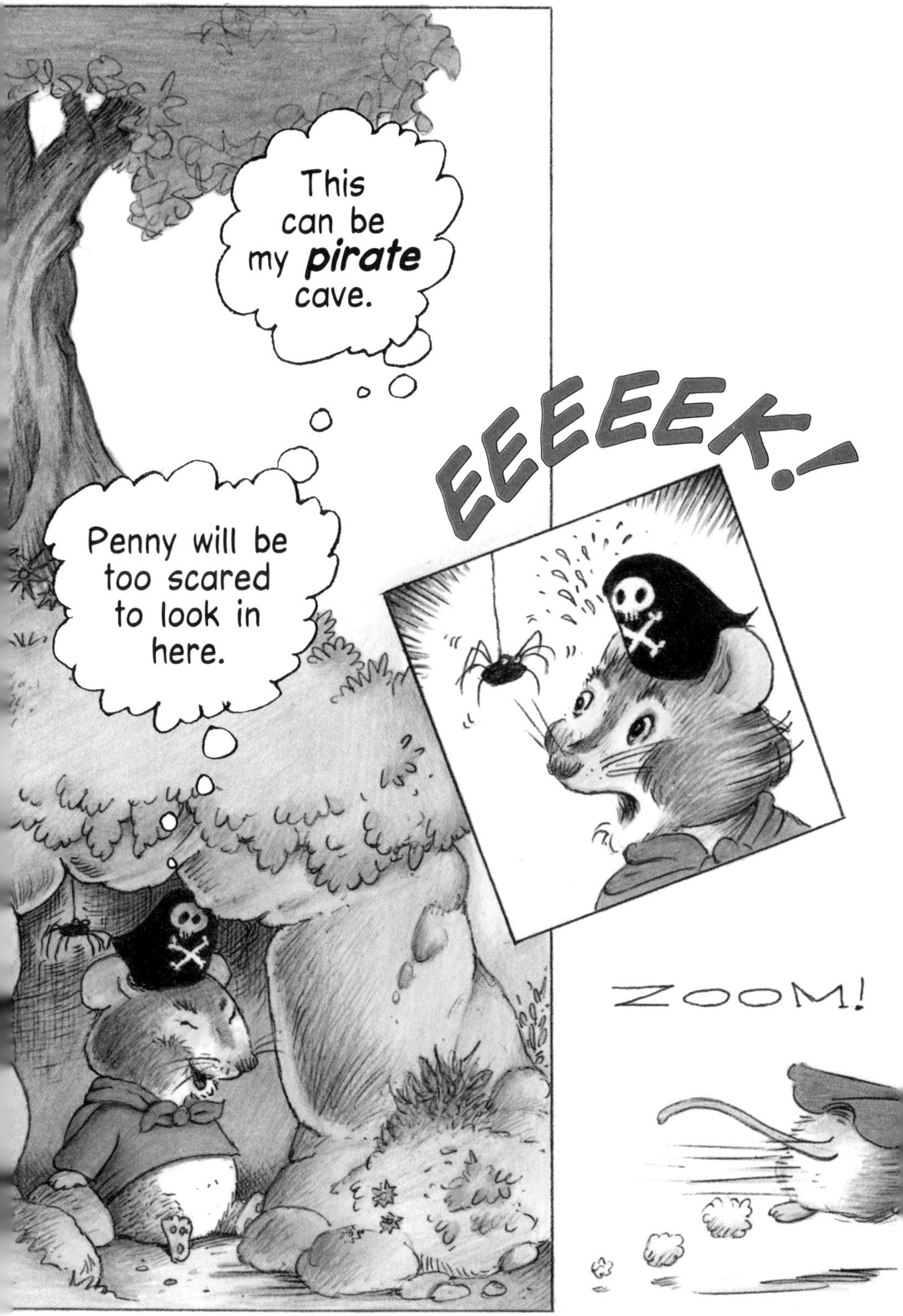
This can be my *pirate* cave.
Penny will be too scared to look in here.
EEEEEK!
ZOOM!

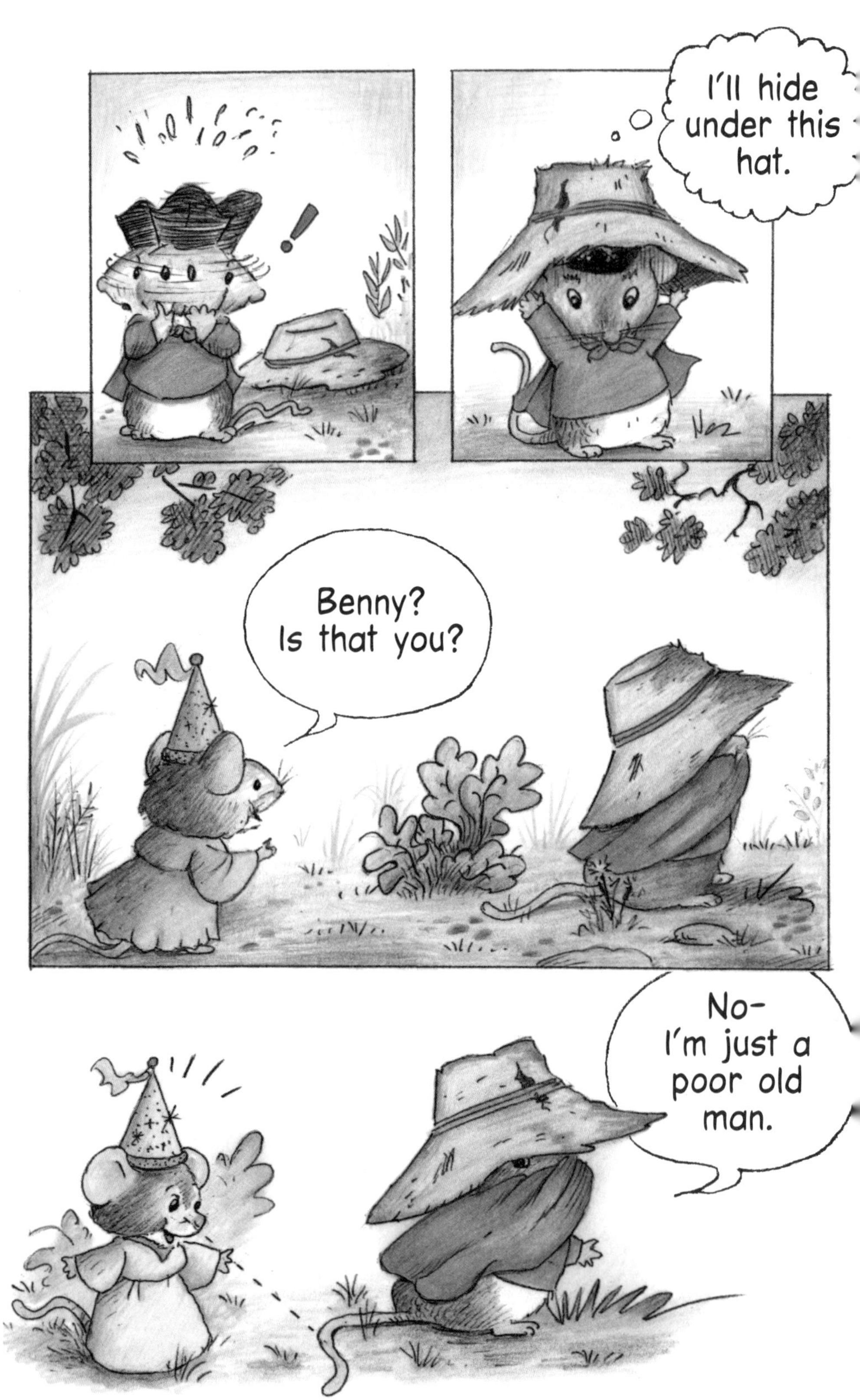
I'll hide under this hat.
Benny? Is that you?
No- I'm just a poor old man.

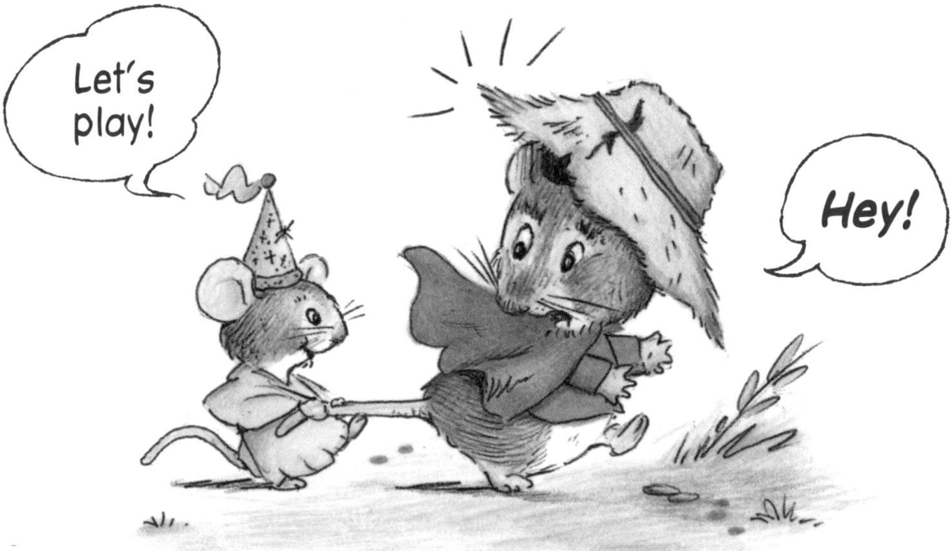
Let's play!
Hey!

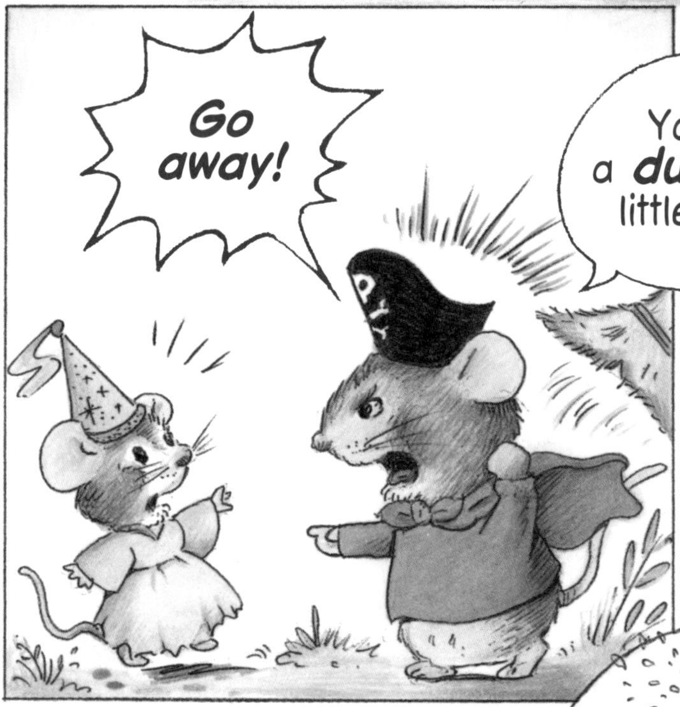
Go away!
You are a **dumb,** bad little sister!

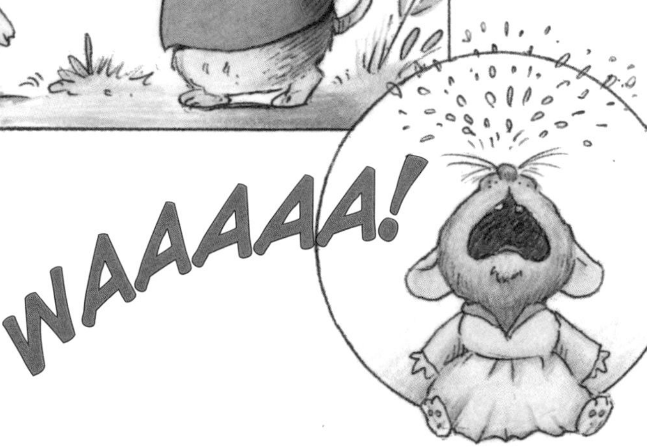
WAAAAA!

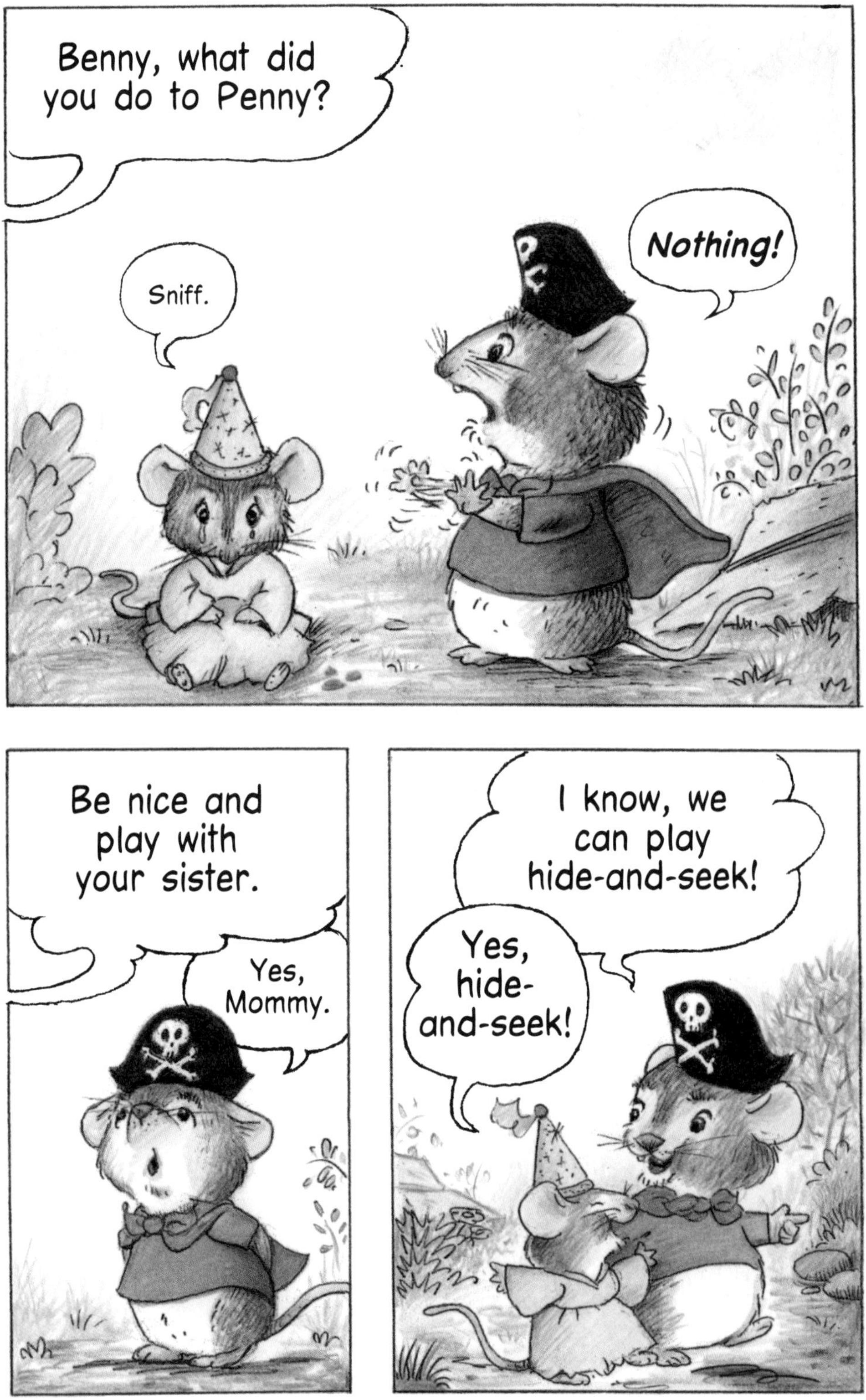
Benny, what did you do to Penny?
Sniff.
Nothing!
Be nice and play with your sister.
Yes, Mommy.
I know, we can play hide-and-seek!
Yes, hide-and-seek!

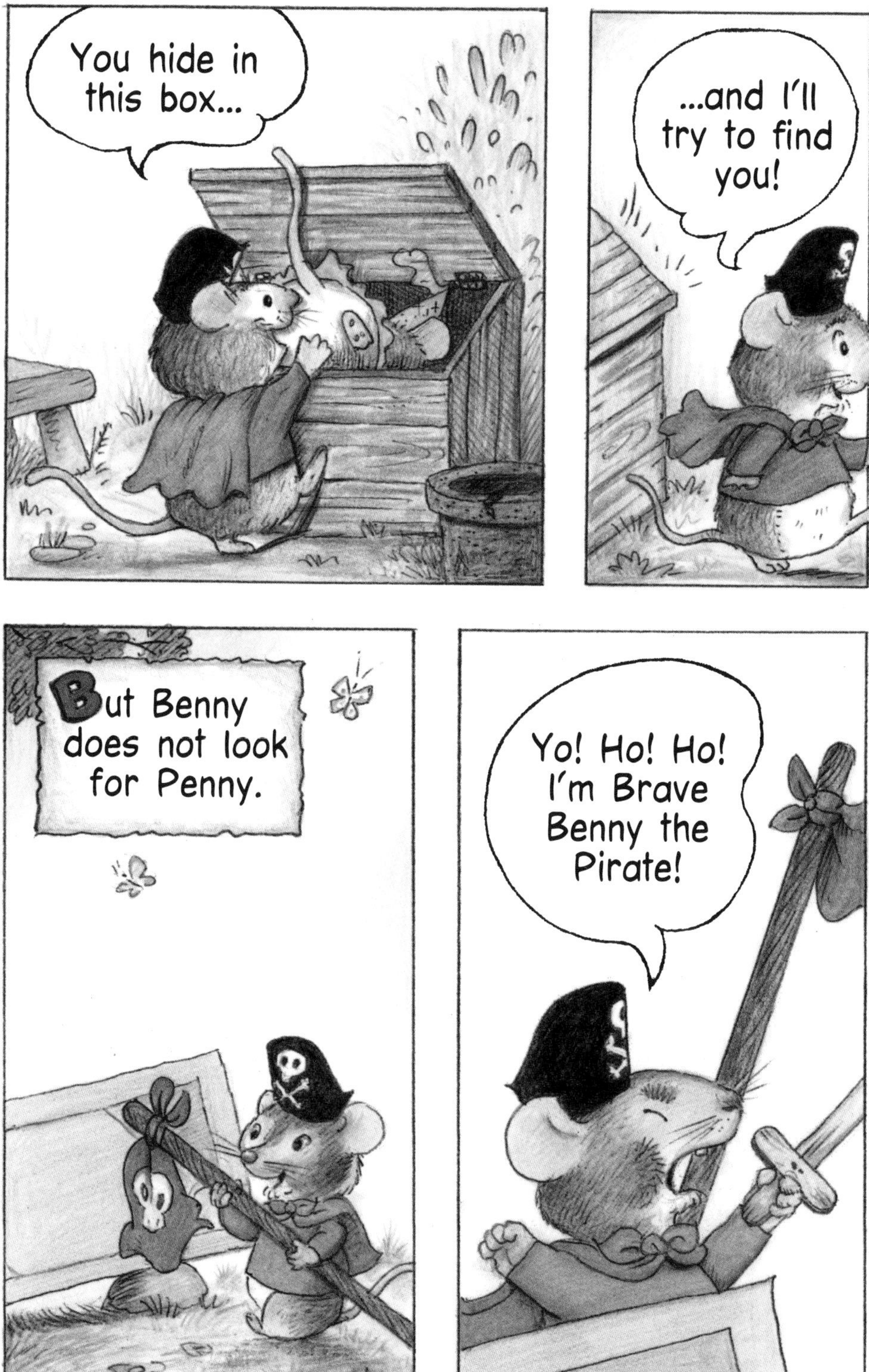
You hide in this box...
...and I'll try to find you!
But Benny does not look for Penny.
Yo! Ho! Ho! I'm Brave Benny the Pirate!

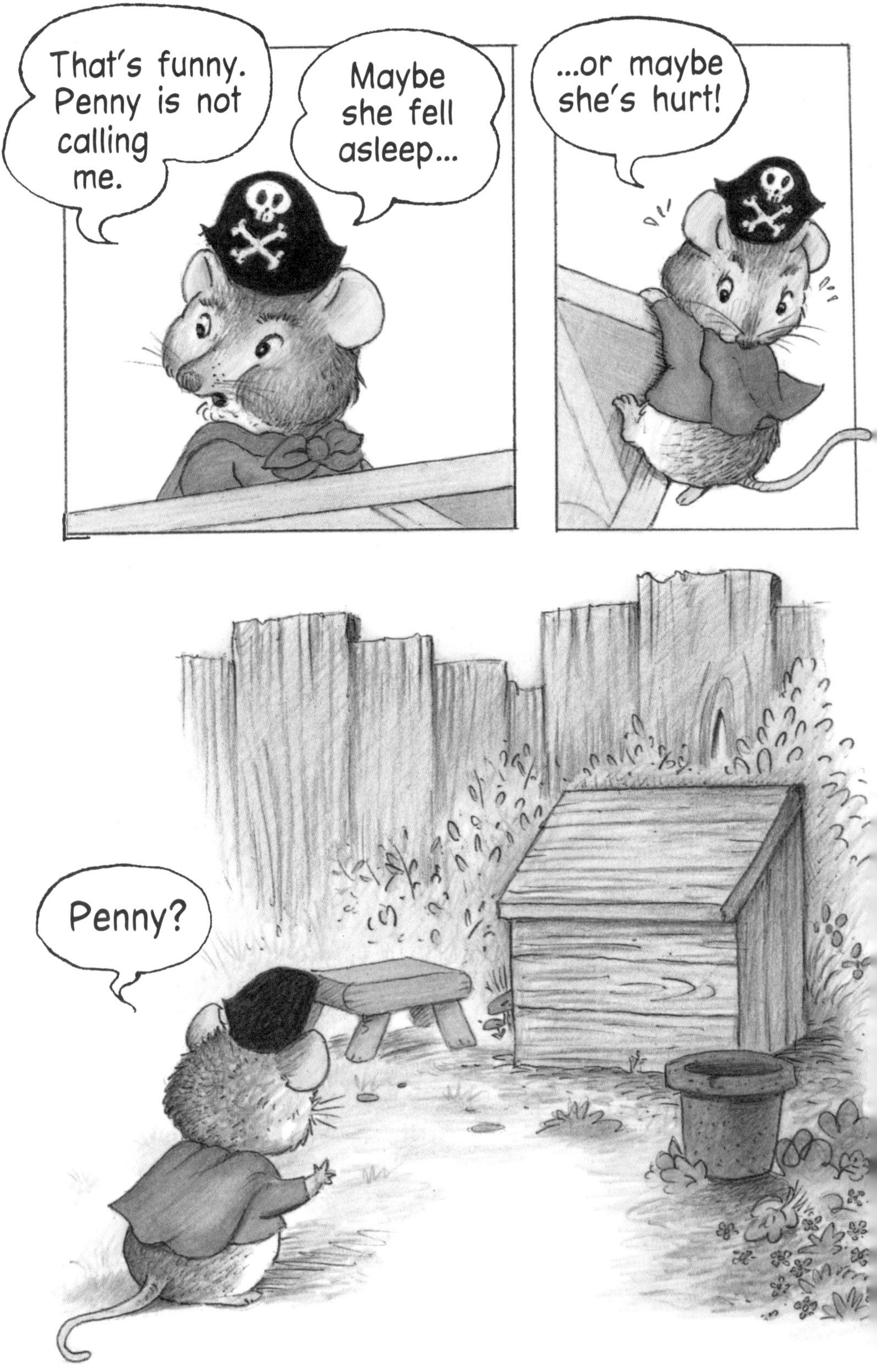
That's funny. Penny is not calling me.
Maybe she fell asleep...
...or maybe she's hurt!
Penny?

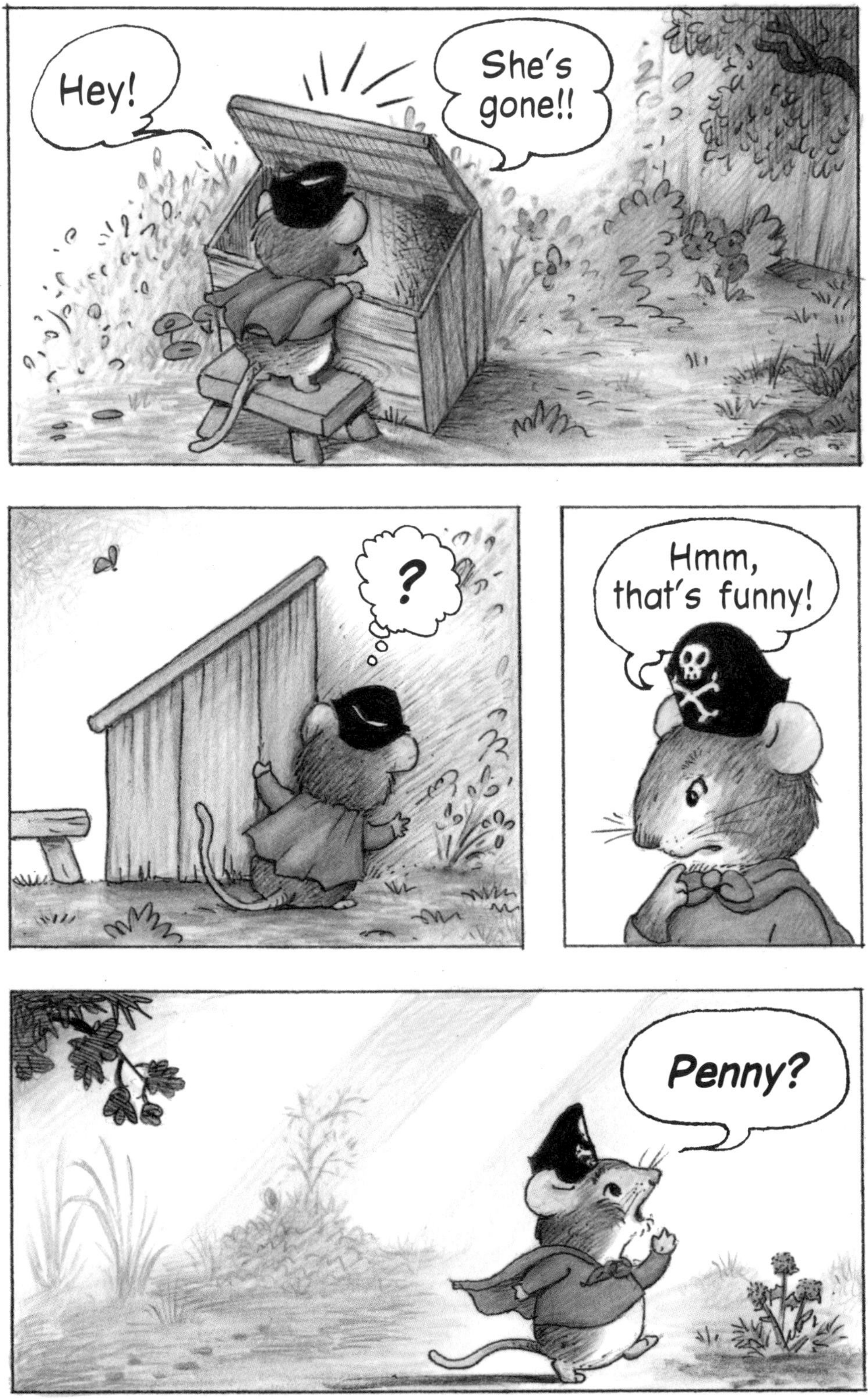

Hey!
She's gone!!
?
Hmm, that's funny!
Penny?

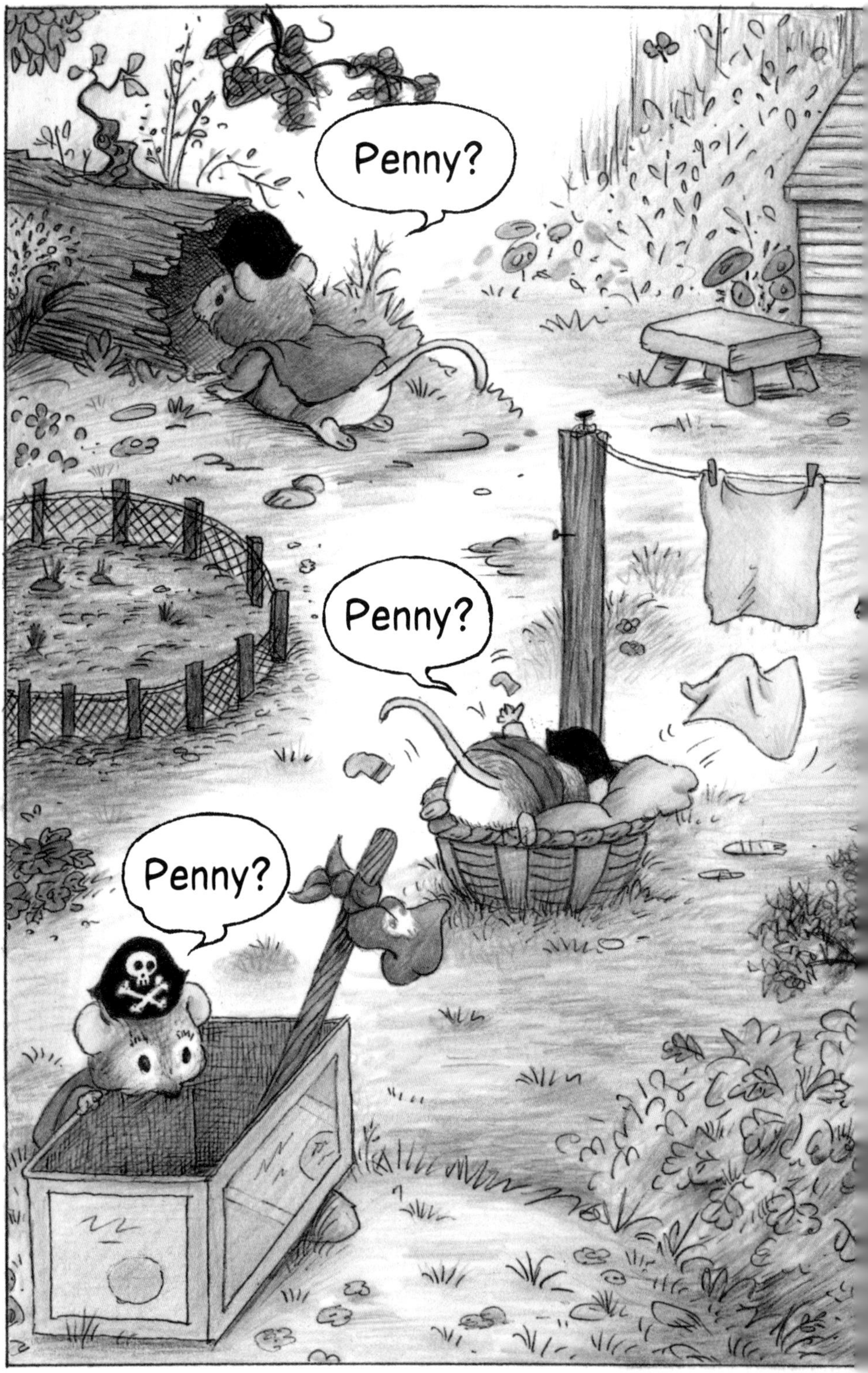
Penny?
Penny?
Penny?

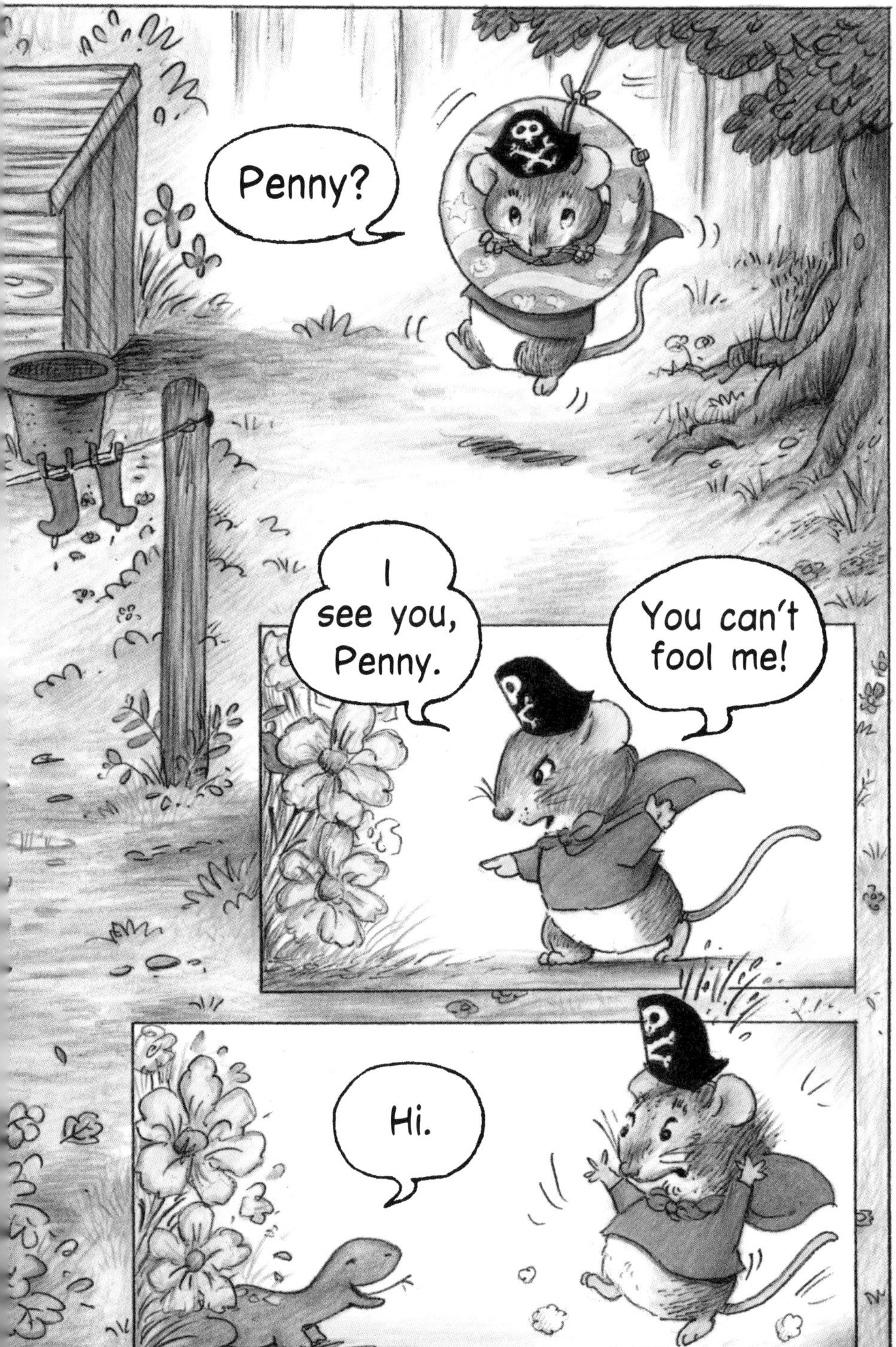
Penny?
I see you, Penny.
You can't fool me!
Hi.

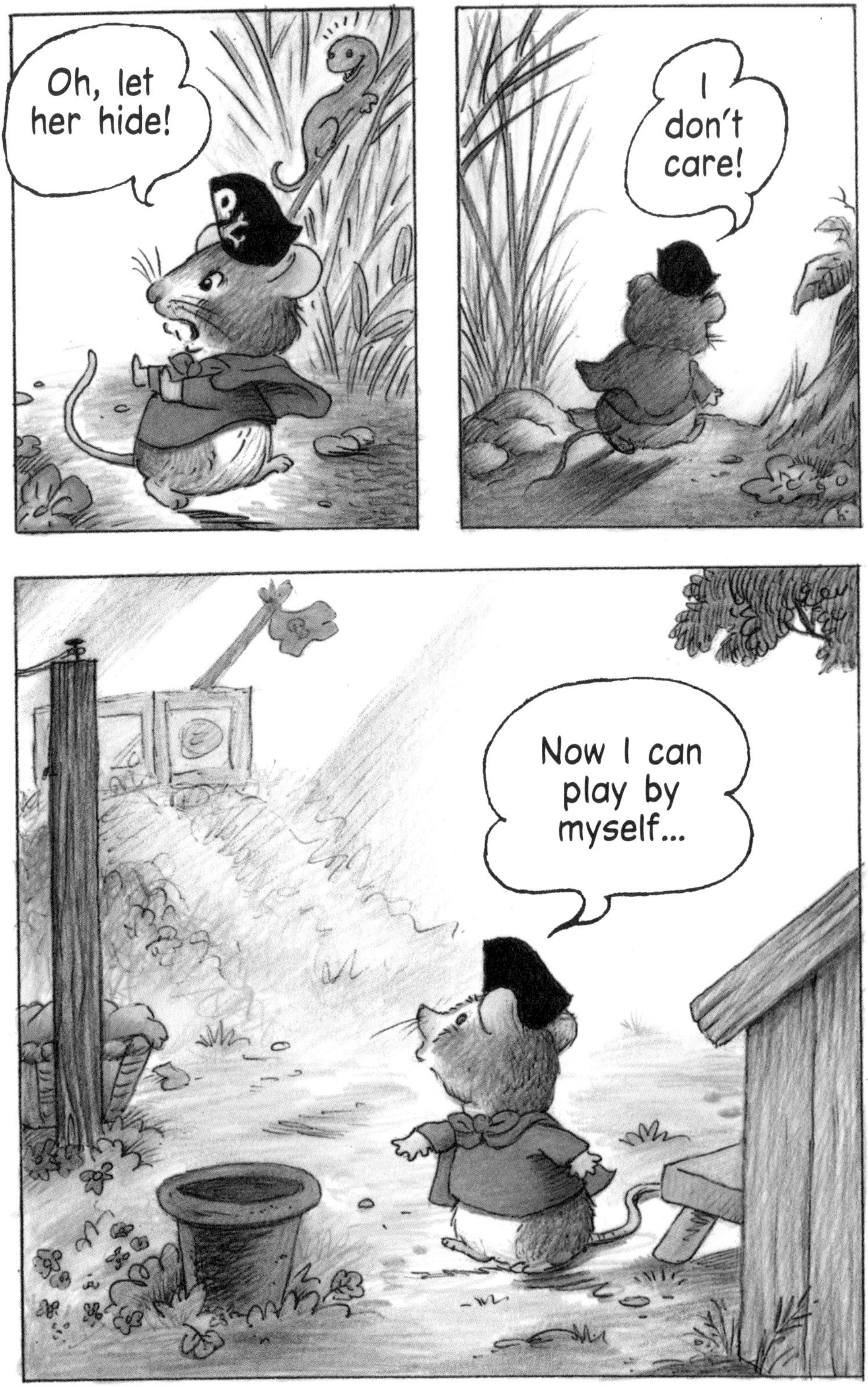
Oh, let her hide!
I don't care!
Now I can play by myself...

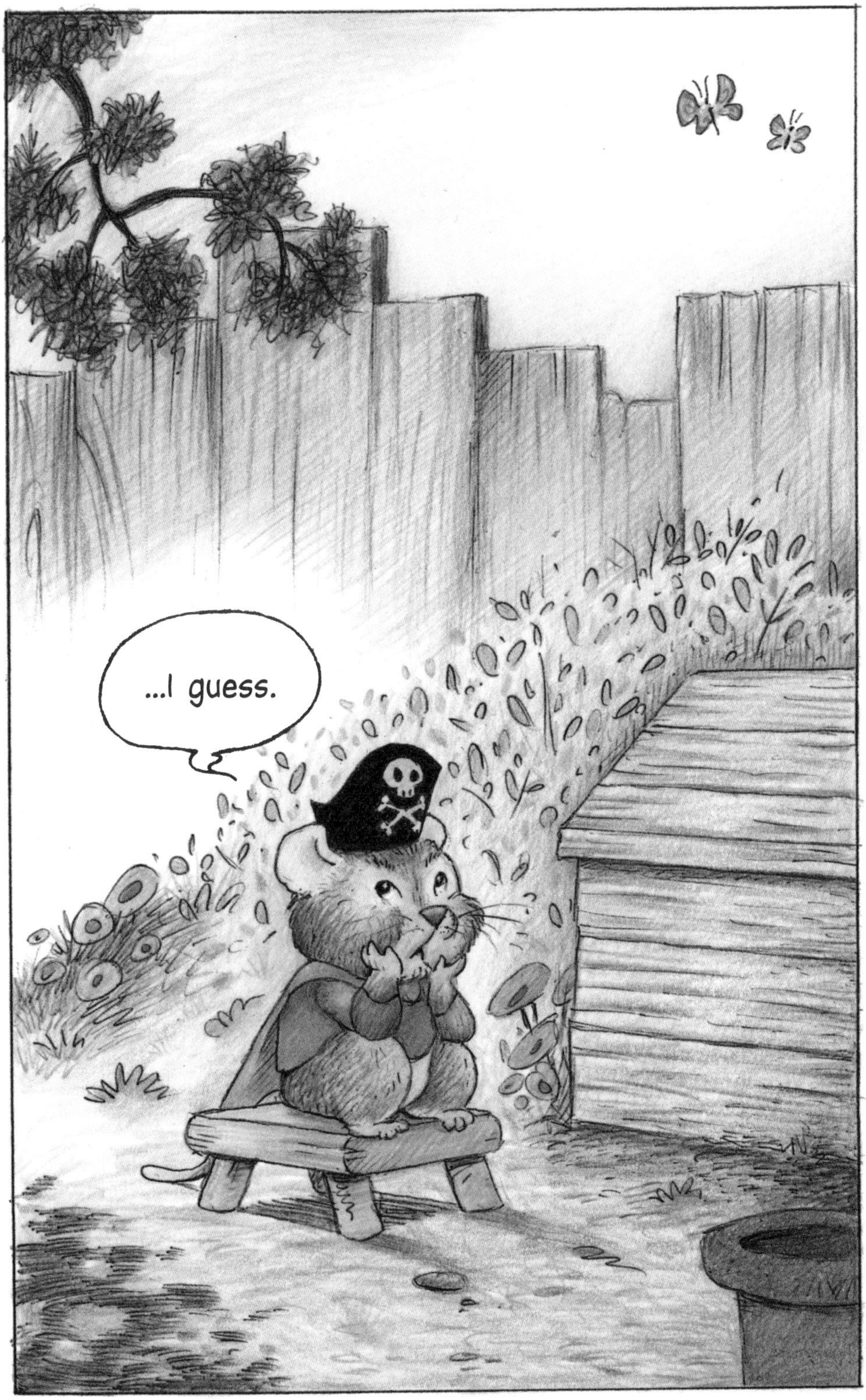
...I guess.

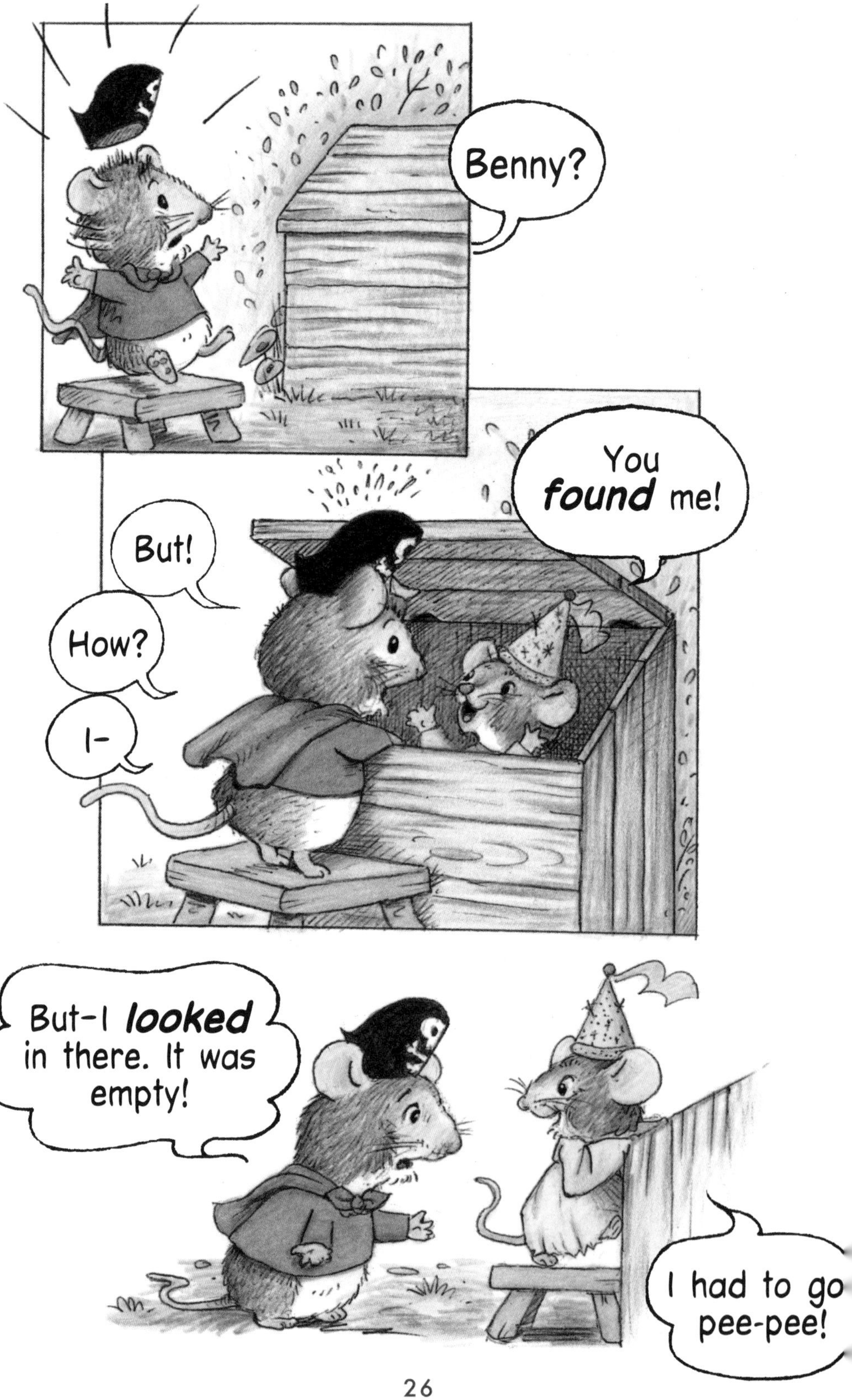
Benny?
You *found* me!
But!
How?
I-
But-I *looked* in there. It was empty!
I had to go pee-pee!

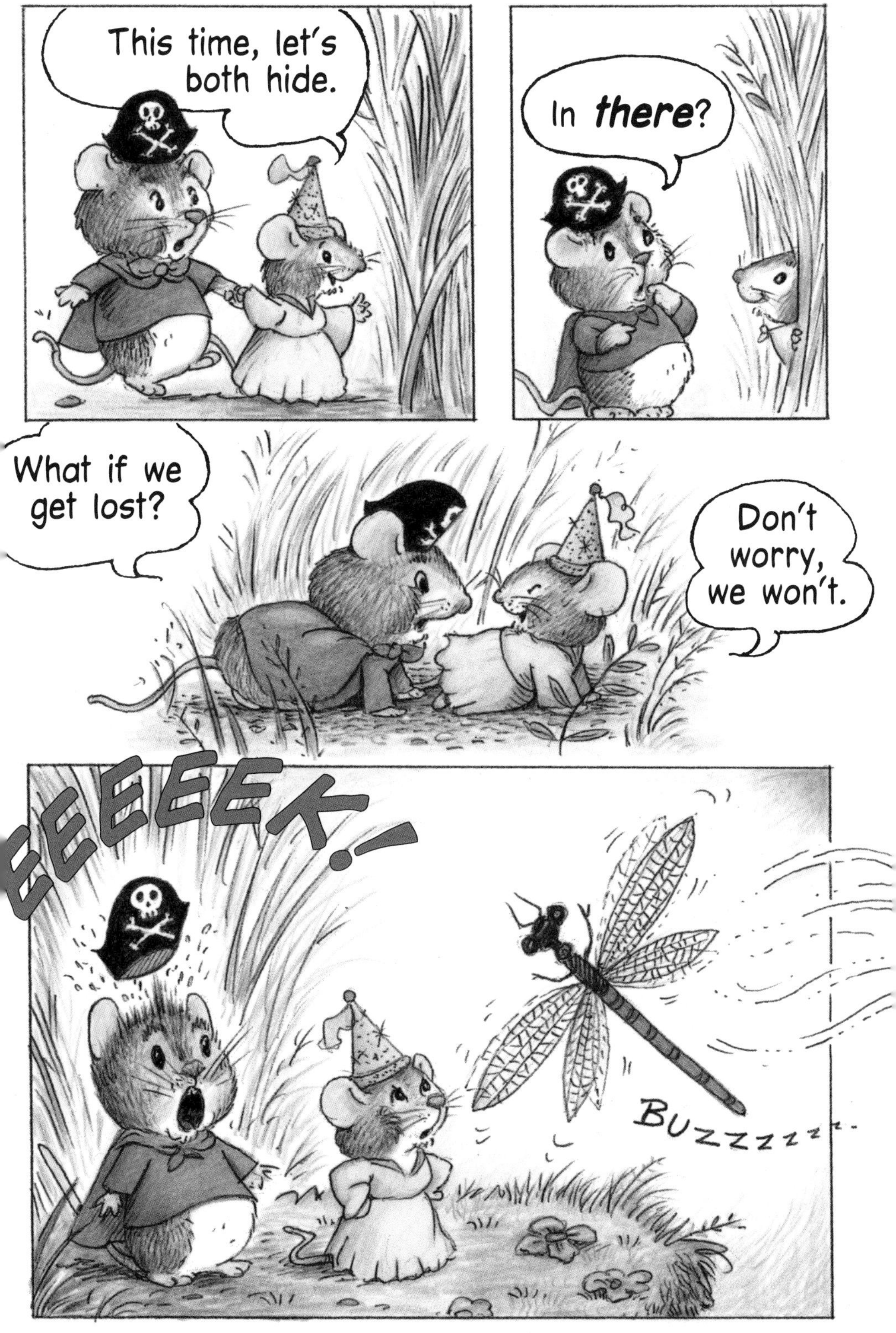
This time, let's both hide.
In *there*?
What if we get lost?
Don't worry, we won't.
EEEEEK!
BUZZZZZZ

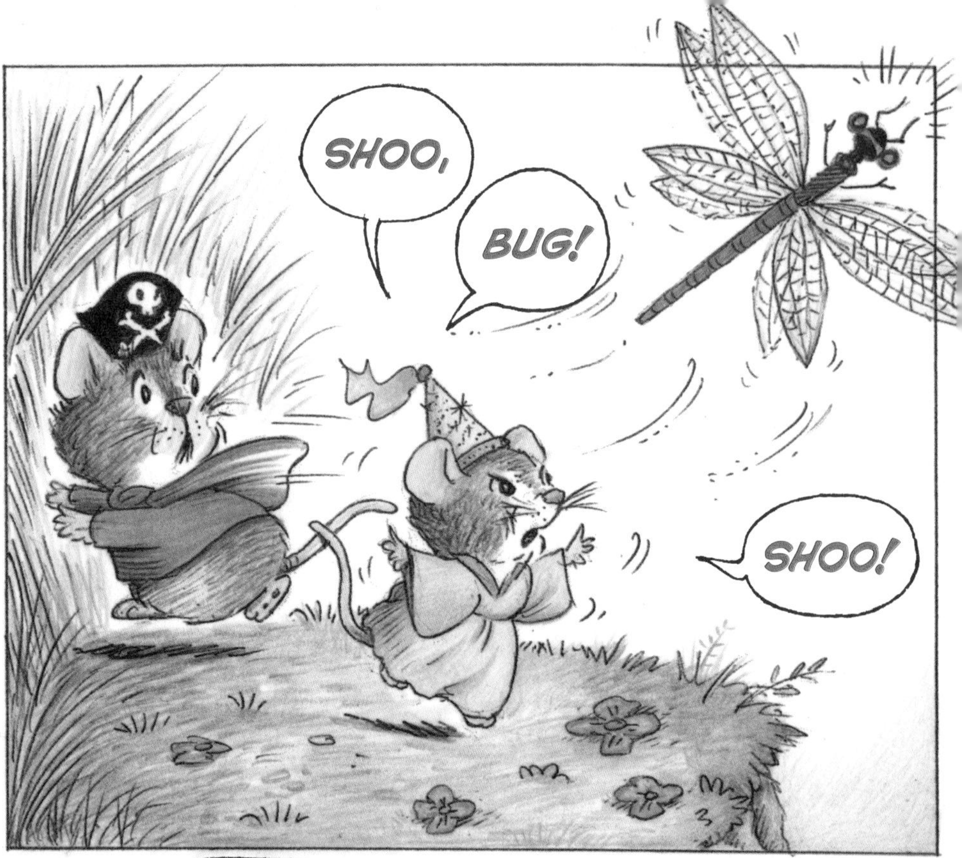
SHOO,
BUG!
SHOO!

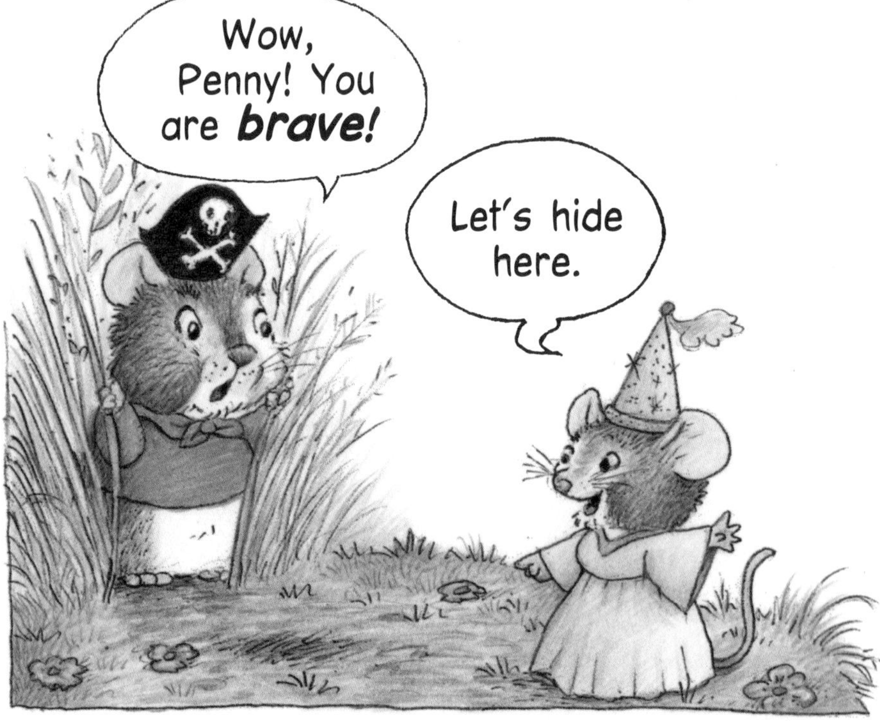
Wow, Penny! You are **brave!**
Let's hide here.

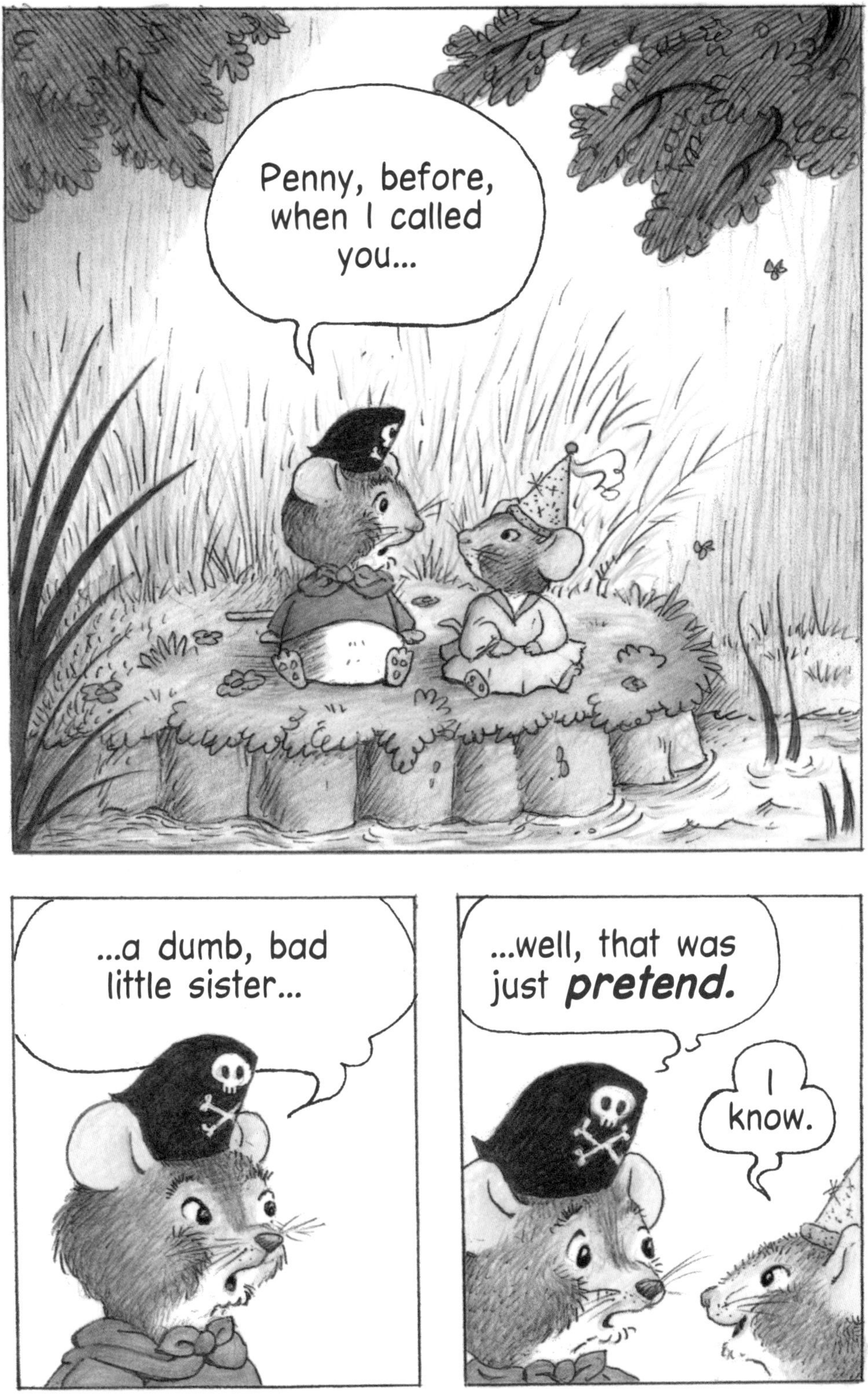
Penny, before, when I called you...
...a dumb, bad little sister...
...well, that was just ***pretend.***
I know.

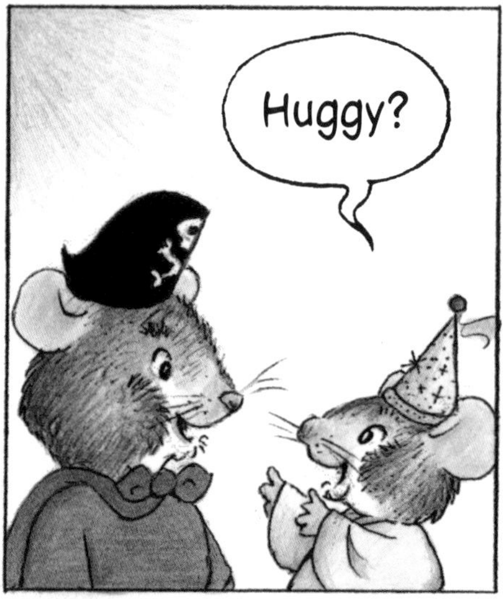
Huggy?

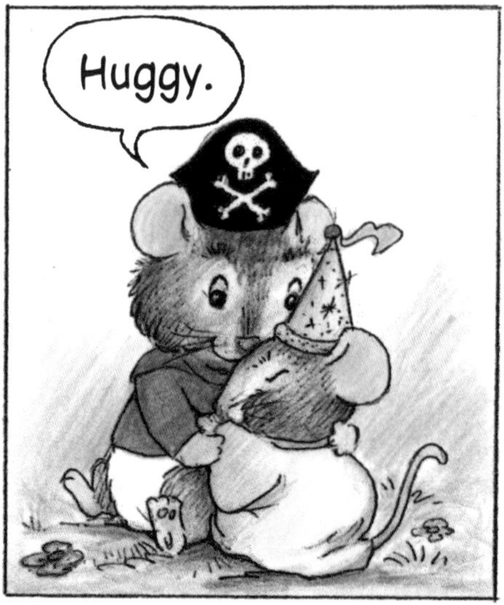
Huggy.

And where are Benny and Penny now?

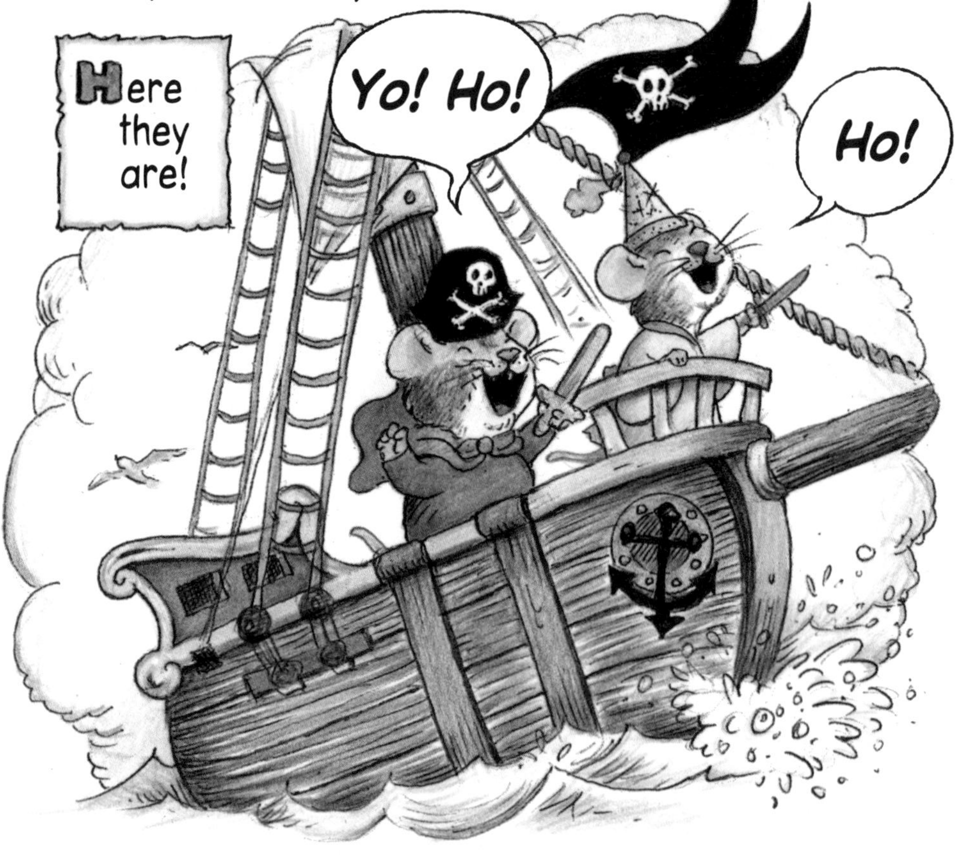
Here they are!
Yo! Ho!
Ho!

# THE END

## ABOUT THE AUTHOR

***Geoffrey*** grew up in San Francisco, where he still lives. From an early age, he and his younger brother Rory wrote and illustrated stories for one another.

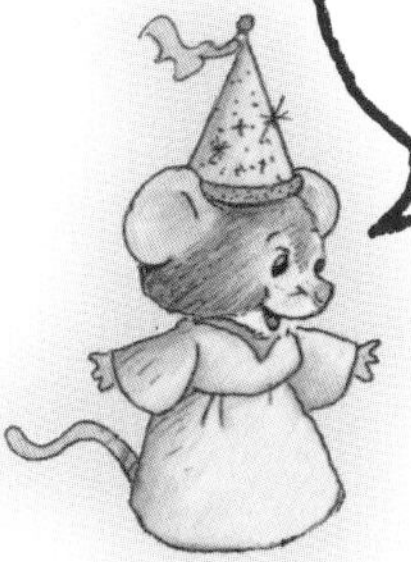

Geoffrey says, "Like ***Benny*** I often wanted to play alone. But when I gave in to Rory's demands that I play with him, I was always glad that I did." Both Geoffrey and Rory grew up to be artists.

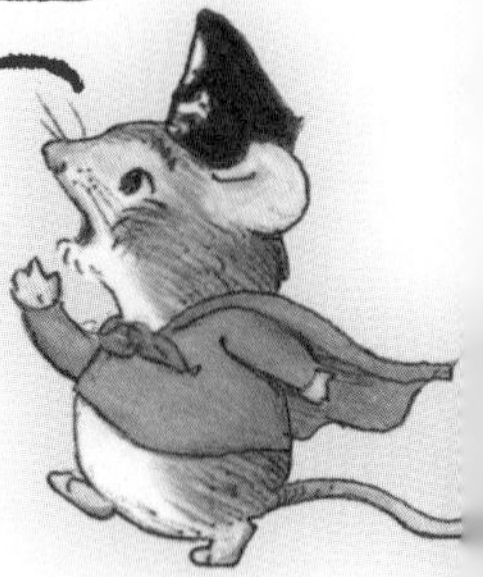

Geoffrey has written and illustrated over forty children's books, among them the classic *Bear By Himself* and *When the Wind Blew* by Margaret Wise Brown. He is the author of the extremely successful series of early readers *Otto and Uncle Tooth.*